COLORFUL
DRAGONS FAR AND NEAR

BY DAN PEELER

AND

CHARLIE ROSE

PUBLISHED BY
DEBE INK
HOUSTON TEXAS

Prunk is a very young Dragon
His wings are like a bat

Fetita's wings are on her back. Some Dragons are made like that.

They love to hear Vladimir's stories
about all their dragon relations.

Stories of dragons who live next door and others in far-away nations.

Cosmina, an Argus Dragon,
has wings like a peacock's tail.

Tanarul has no wings at all,
but, rides the wind like a sail.

The Padure looks just like a tree
with leaves and finger branches.

Viorica loves to fly through clouds
and wave to cows on ranches.

A Dragon called the Cockatrice
crows a red rooster's call.

Fetita said, "that seems so weird;
not like a Dragon at all.

Vladimir smiled and shook his head.
"Our family's scope is wide."

"The Bunyip has a bulldog's face,
with scales along his side."

A Chinese Dragon, like a snake,
swims the far-east sky.

The Japanese Bird-Dragon
flaps feathered wings to fly.

Lou, the Dragon, is so tall;
much taller than a house.

The Dragon, Urk, is very small;
small as the smallest mouse.

In the mountains of Tibet,
Nimu shines his scales.

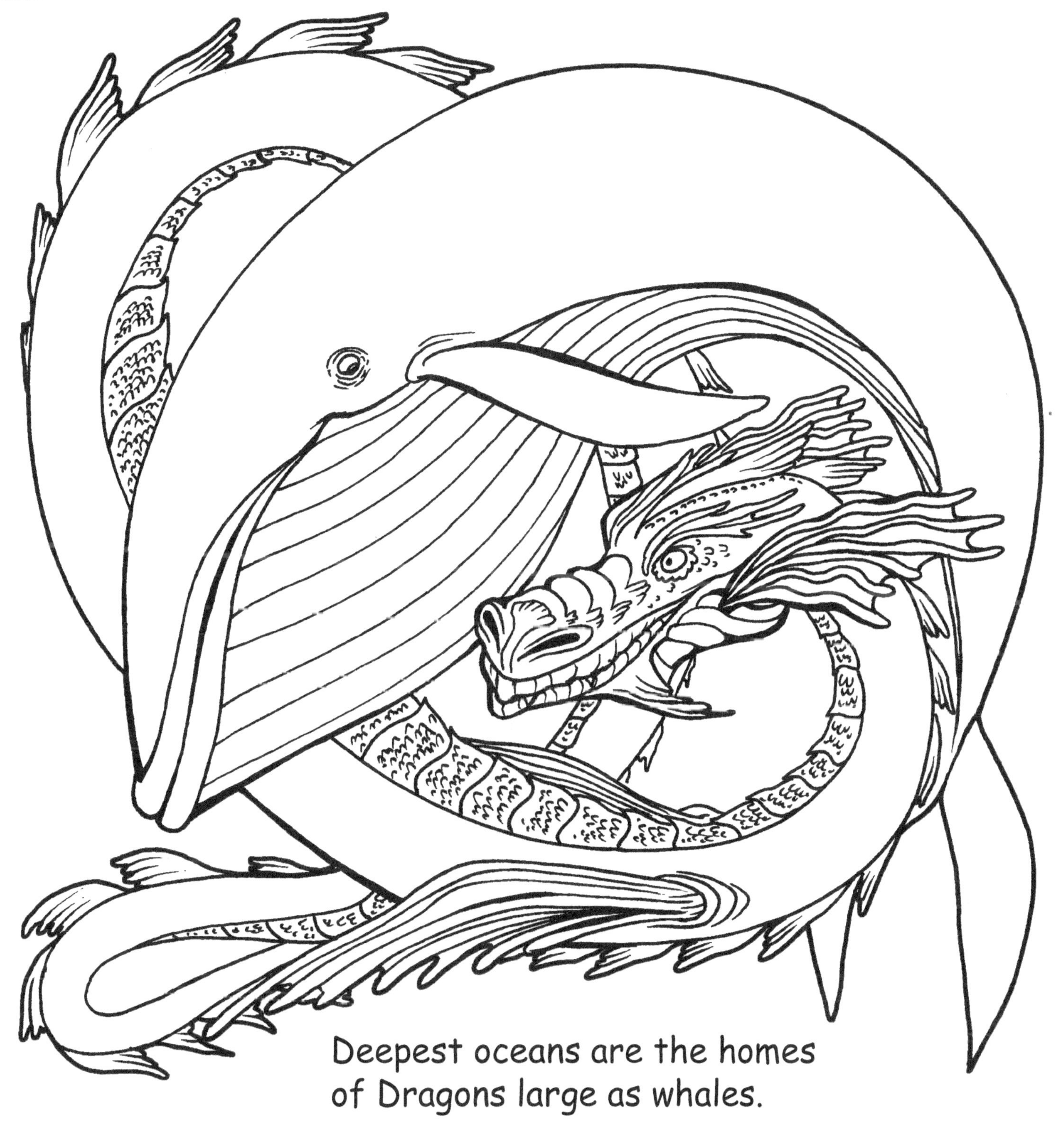

Deepest oceans are the homes
of Dragons large as whales.

Some Dragons live in great icebergs
and float the Arctic Seas.

Others live in jungle lands
with coconuts on trees.

Sirrush makes his home in deserts,
where hot sandstorms blow.

Bogdan loves the deep dark
caves, with crystal rocks below.

Some Dragons' backs are spiked with horns,
just like a porcupine.

The leaf-back Dragon's wings are soft, and have a satin shine.

Some young Dragons read for days
from books with lots of words.

"Others play their Dragon Games
and run outside in herds."

"They are lots of colors," said Prunk,
"Like purples, greens, and reds!"

"Fetita said, "Some have smooth
scales, or horns grow on their heads."

"Most dragons have a single head,
like Prunk's, and yours, and mine.

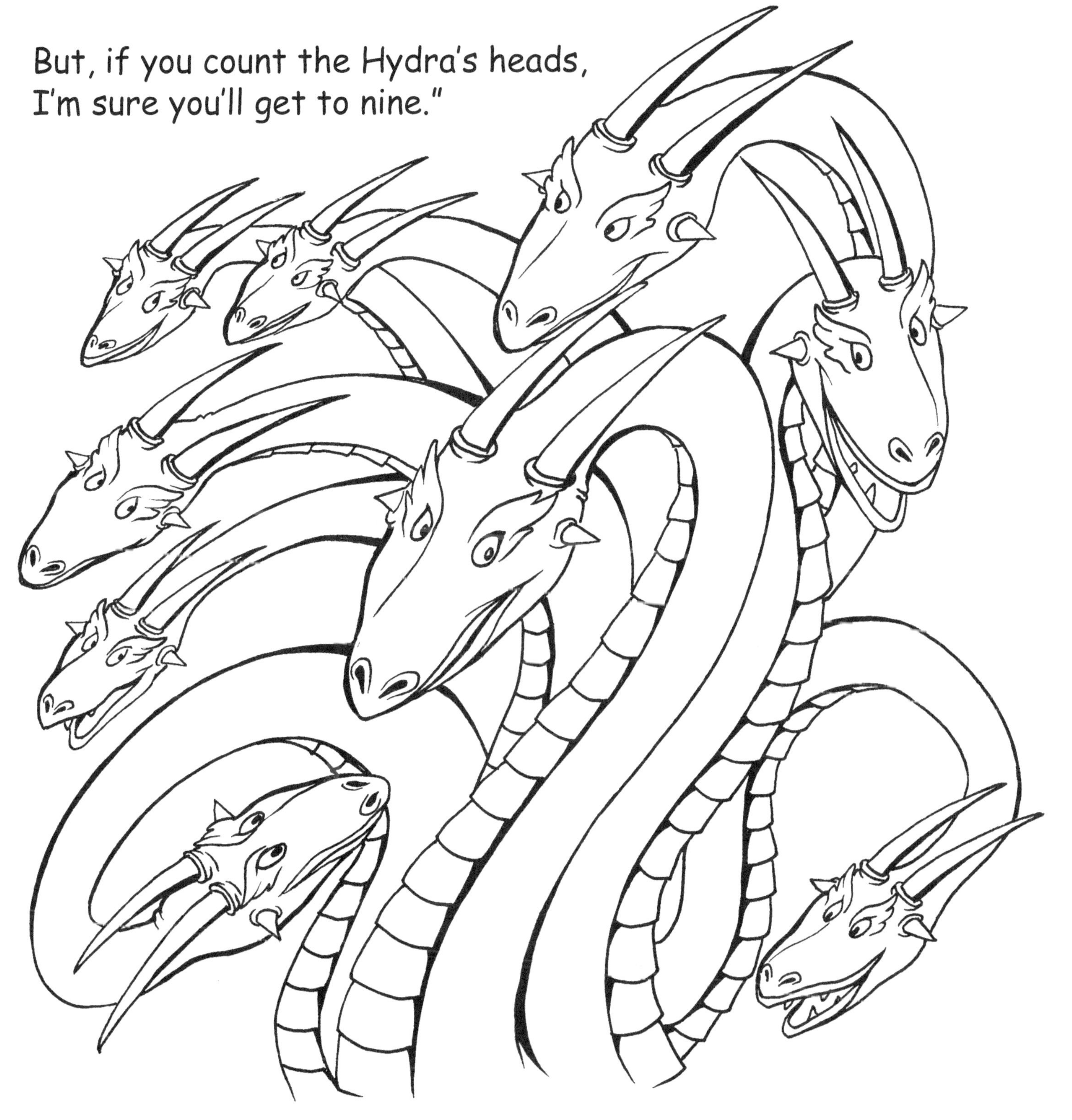
But, if you count the Hydra's heads,
I'm sure you'll get to nine."

Fetita said, "Nine heads? I just can't wait to tell my brother!"

"I think we understand," said Prunk.
"No Dragon is like another."

Fetita said, "So many kinds of Dragons I don't know!"

"We've just begun," said Vladimir.
"The list can only grow!"

"I'm really glad," Fetita smiled,
"that most don't look like me!"

"If we all looked and thought alike,
how boring life would be!"

Make a DRAGON Instructions

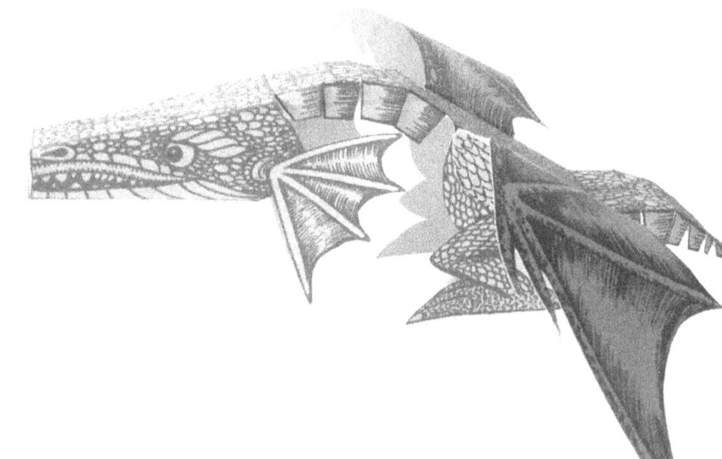

Materials needed . . .

1. One sheet of color card stock (your choice of color)
2. Scissors
3. Glue dots, double sided tape, or white glue

Assembly . . .

1. Copy Dragon on color card stock
2. Cut out the five printed sections labeled A, B, C, D, E
   - Remember: Do not to cut off the tabs.
3. Fold Dragon (A) together on all straight fold lines, including tabs.
4. Glue the folded front of the nose into the folded face.
5. Glue overlapping chin flaps together.
6. Glue wings (B, C) on sides of body, even with top of back.
7. Glue wing scale pieces (D, E) on each side under wings to cover wing tabs.
8. Fold neck and tail up from body.
9. Fold head up at neck.
10. For a realistic pose, bend neck, wings and tail into curves.

Copy as many as you like and make a whole family of Dragons!

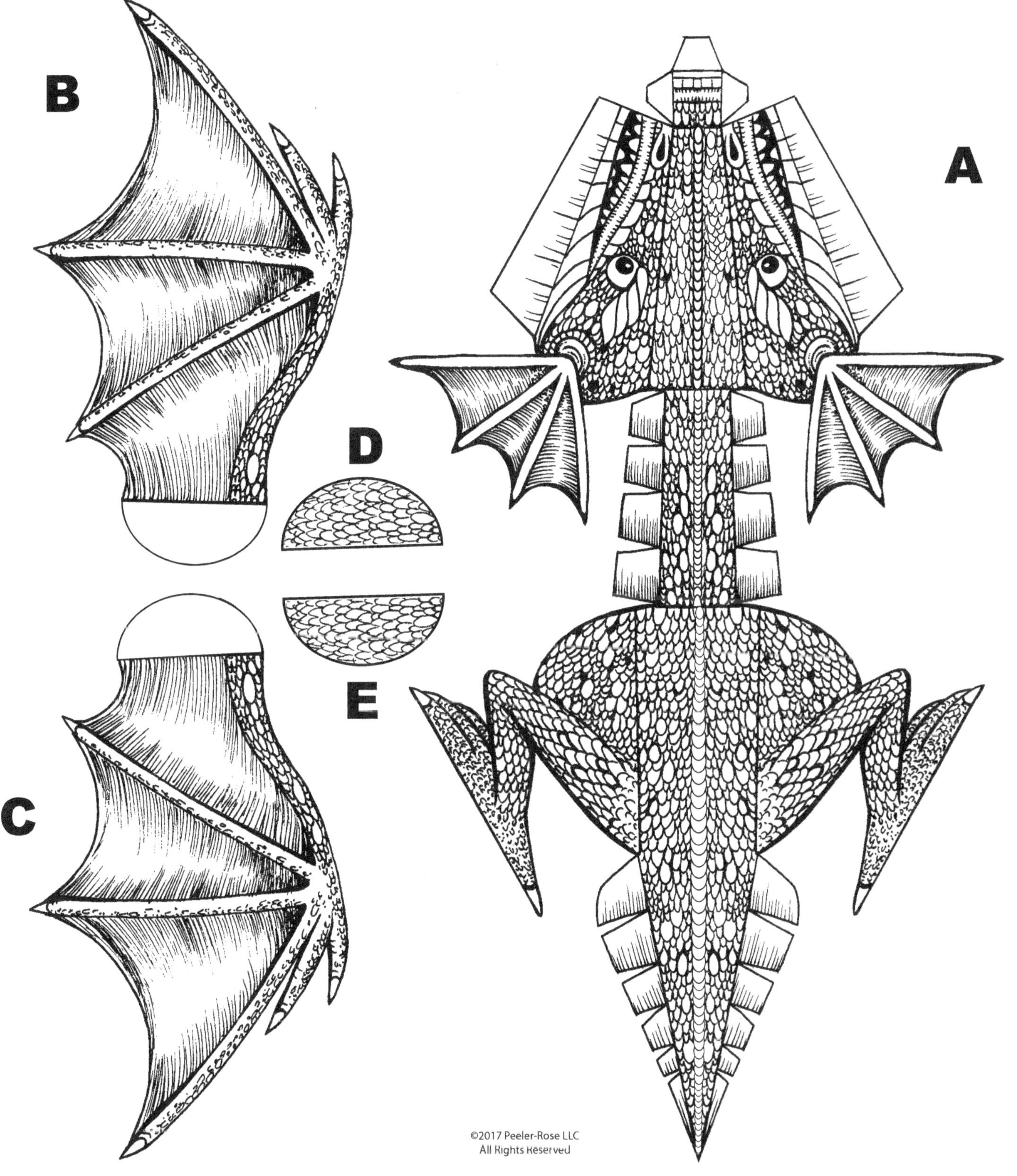

B
D
E
C
A

Colorful Dragons Far and Near
© Copyright 2017
Peeler Rose Productions, LLC
Dallas Texas
All Rights Reserved

ISBN 978-1-946182-97-5
Soft Cover

ISBN 978-1-946182-98-2
Hard Cover

Book and cover designed & illustrated by
Dan Peeler & Charlie Rose

Published by Debe Ink.
www.debeink.com
An imprint of
John M. Hardy Publishing Co.
www.johnhardypublishing.com
Houston Texas

www.ingramcontent.com/pod-product-compliance
Lightning Source LLC
Chambersburg PA
CBHW080726210726
48292CB00017B/2970